To Lori, Shelley and Kristi, who love their Vancouver swims—even in frigid waters. Special thanks also to Tiffany for being an extra set of eyes and ears.—KLW

To Philly—the most patient man in the world.—CL

Text copyright © 2018 by Kari-Lynn Winters Illustrations copyright © 2018 by Christina Leist

Published in Canada and in the US in 2018.

Cataloguing and publication data available from the British Library.

Book design by Elisa Gutiérrez • The text of this book is set in Leticia Bumstead.

10 9 8 7 6 5 4 3 2 1

Printed and bound in Korea on ancient-forest-friendly paper.

MIX
Paper from responsible sources
FSC® C023083

The publisher thanks Hilary Leung for her editorial assistance.

The publisher thanks the Government of Canada, the Canada Council for the Arts and Livres Canada Books for their financial support. We also thank the Government of the Province of British Columbia for the financial support we have received through the Book Publishing Tax Credit program and the British Columbia Arts Council.

LIBRARY AND ARCHIVES CANADA
CATALOGUING IN PUBLICATION

Winters, Kari-Lynn, 1969-, author
    On my swim / Kari-Lynn Winters ; illustrated by Christina Leist.

(On my walk series)
ISBN 978-1-926890-16-6 (hardcover)

    I. Leist, Christina, illustrator II. Title.

PS8645.I5745O4985   2018
jC813'.6   C2017-907884-4

Canada

Canada Council
for the Arts

Conseil des Arts
du Canada

BRITISH
COLUMBIA
ARTS COUNCIL
Supported by the Province of British Columbia

Kari-Lynn Winters

On My Swim

illustrated by **Christina Leist**

Vancouver • London

On my swim,

my summer swim,

I hear the breeze,

and see a bird,

fishery-fish,
fishery-fish.

I feel the sand,

squishery-squish,
squishery-squish,

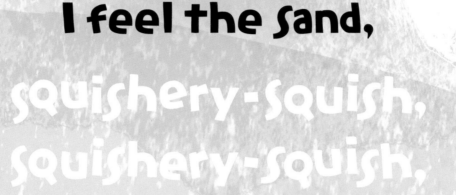

and a wave,

splishery-splish,
splishery-splish.

Uh-oh!

Time to go!

swish, swish,

Splish, Splish,

squishery-squish,

squishery-squish,

fish, fish,

all dried off.